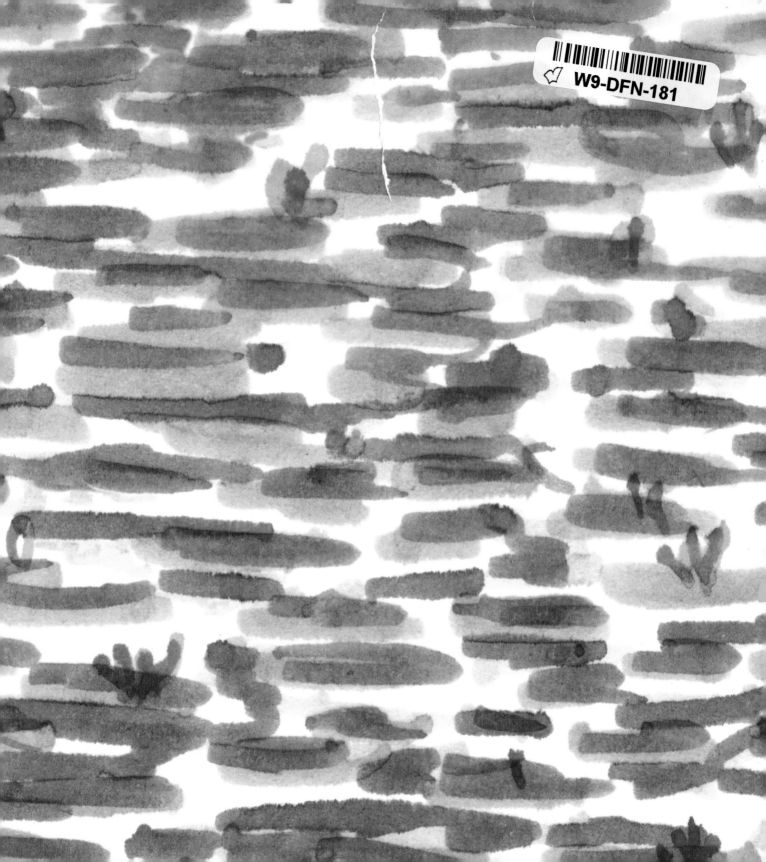

Thank you to all my family and friends,
who continually help me, guide me, support me and mostly,
encourage me to follow this wondrous dream now turned reality.

This book was illustrated by Juan Carlos Casas

First edition of a series 2009

Library of Congress Cataloging-in-Publication
Data is available
ISBN# 978-0-980-1367-1-5

2fish, Inc. NY
www.thinkthenjump.com

Printed in Singapore

The Careless Frog

A Think...Then Jump™ Series

by
Dana L. Perri

Illustrated by
Juan Carlos Casas

2fish, Inc. NY

Rana was hopping all through the woods,
leaping and jumping as fast as he could.

He jumped around from here to there,
bouncing about without even a care.

Rana leapt so high that he lost his footing.

He fell into the mud which splattered
like pudding!

His next big leap landed him atop a red flower.

He crushed all her petals with his big, mighty power.

Singing and hopping and leaping his way,
he left dust and destruction wherever he may.

The next leap he took flew over
Two Tooth the Beaver...

Who was busily using his front teeth
like a cleaver.

The breeze and the noise that Rana's leap caused scared Two Tooth so much that the log stuck to his claws.

Now Rana was off with super lightning speed.
He jumped up and jumped over,
spilling a bucket of feed.

Poor Peachy the Pig rolled over in fear,
her legs up in the air,
food piled up to her ear!

Chaos and confusion were left by Rana's journey.
Everyone thought it was the work of Ferret Brown Bernie.

But Lulu knew who could cause such disaster.
She flew overhead from pond clear to pasture.

And all through the forest, as far as she could see,
she found friends and nature covered in debris.

Now Lulu the bird knew just where to look.
She flew on down by the side of the brook.

Right by the water, she found Rana the Frog,
resting so comfortably on a long, dry log.

So happy to see her he yelled out, "Hi Lulu!
Pull up a log. Tell me what's new!"

She realized he didn't know the mess he had made,
as he asked, "Care to rest for awhile, you look a bit crazed?"

She spoke softly but firmly, "I'm very upset, my friend.
You have carelessly romped through the forest end to end."

"What do you mean?" he asked a bit confused.
"I was just having fun and keeping quite amused."

Lulu asked,
"When you landed on the flower with all of your might,
you crushed her red petals...

Did you think that was right?"

"When you scared Two Tooth so badly
that his claws got stuck,

Did you think that was just his own bad luck?"

"And what about poor Peachy the Pig?
Do you think she is off dancing the jig?

No, she is sitting around with a big, old pout.
'Cause her pen is a mess with her food spread about!"

Rana looked up with such a sad face.
He had no idea he made a mess of the place.

He sat and thought of the things he had done,
not realizing he was careless or hurting anyone.

His jumping about was meant to be fun.
Yet his actions were thoughtless,
no thought,
Not One!

Lulu smiled at Rana, who of course now knew,
that we must all be careful of the things that we do.

So, Rana went back through the forest again.
"I'm sorry!" he said to each and every friend.

"Now let's go back so that I can see,
how to clean up the mess that was caused by me."

"What a day, what a day,
beautiful in every way."

Questions to ponder

What does 'being careless' mean?

Why was Lulu upset?

Name some of the ways that Rana was careless.

How do you think Peachy the Pig and Two Tooth the Beaver felt?

What did Rana learn?

What did Rana do at the end of the story?

Have you ever been careless? What happened?

Why was it a beautiful day?

think... then jump™